Blastoff! Readers are carefully developed by literacy experts to build reading stamina and move students toward fluency by combining standards-based content with developmentally appropriate text.

Level 1 provides the most support through repetition of high-frequency words, light text, predictable sentence patterns, and strong visual support.

Level 2 offers early readers a bit more challenge through varied sentences, increased text load, and text-supportive special features.

Level 3 advances early-fluent readers toward fluency through increased text load, less reliance on photos, advancing concepts, longer sentences, and more complex special features.

★ **Blastoff! Universe**

This edition first published in 2023 by Bellwether Media, Inc.

No part of this publication may be reproduced in whole or in part without written permission of the publisher. For information regarding permission, write to Bellwether Media, Inc., Attention: Permissions Department, 6012 Blue Circle Drive, Minnetonka, MN 55343.

Library of Congress Cataloging-in-Publication Data

Names: Davies, Monika, author.
Title: Egypt / by Monika Davies.
Other titles: Blastoff! readers. 2, Countries of the world.
Description: Minneapolis : Bellwether Media, Inc., 2023. | Series: Blastoff! Readers. Countries of the world | Includes bibliographical references and index. | Audience: Ages 5-8 | Audience: Grades 2-3 | Summary: "Relevant images match informative text in this introduction to Egypt. Intended for students in kindergarten through third grade"– Provided by publisher
Identifiers: LCCN 2022044248 (print) | LCCN 2022044249 (ebook) | ISBN 9798886871296 (library binding) | ISBN 9798886872552 (ebook)
Subjects: LCSH: Egypt–Juvenile literature.
Classification: LCC DT49 .D26 2023 (print) | LCC DT49 (ebook) | DDC 962–dc23/eng/20220913
LC record available at https://lccn.loc.gov/2022044248
LC ebook record available at https://lccn.loc.gov/2022044249

Text copyright © 2023 by Bellwether Media, Inc. BLASTOFF! READERS and associated logos are trademarks and/or registered trademarks of Bellwether Media, Inc.

Editor: Elizabeth Neuenfeldt   Designer: Gabriel Hilger

Printed in the United States of America, North Mankato, MN.

Table of Contents

All About Egypt	4
Land and Animals	6
Life in Egypt	12
Egypt Facts	20
Glossary	22
To Learn More	23
Index	24

All About Egypt

Cairo

Egypt is in northeastern Africa. It is part of the **Middle East**.

Egypt was home to one of the earliest **civilizations**! Its capital is Cairo.

Land and Animals

The Nile River flows through Egypt's **deserts**. The Western Desert is dry and mostly flat. Sandy hills cover the Eastern Desert.

The northeastern Sinai **Peninsula** links Asia and Africa.

Sinai Peninsula

Nile River

Size: 4,132 miles (6,650 kilometers) long

Famous For: one of the longest rivers in the world

Winters in Egypt are cool and mild. Summers are dry and hot.

Little rain falls on Egypt. **Sandstorms** can blow across deserts.

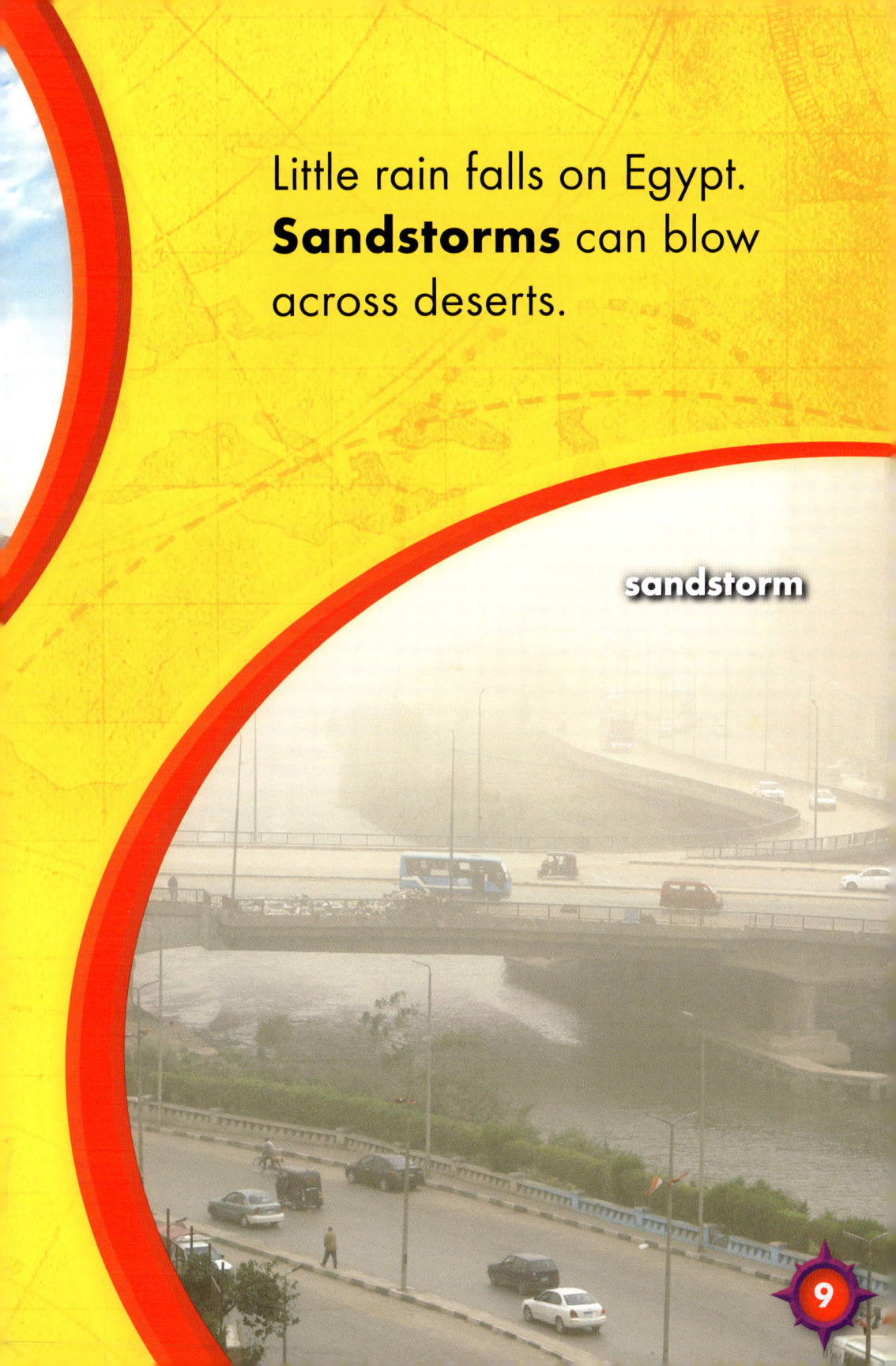

sandstorm

Different animals call Egypt home. Dorcas gazelles walk across deserts. Hooded crows often live in cities.

dorcas gazelles

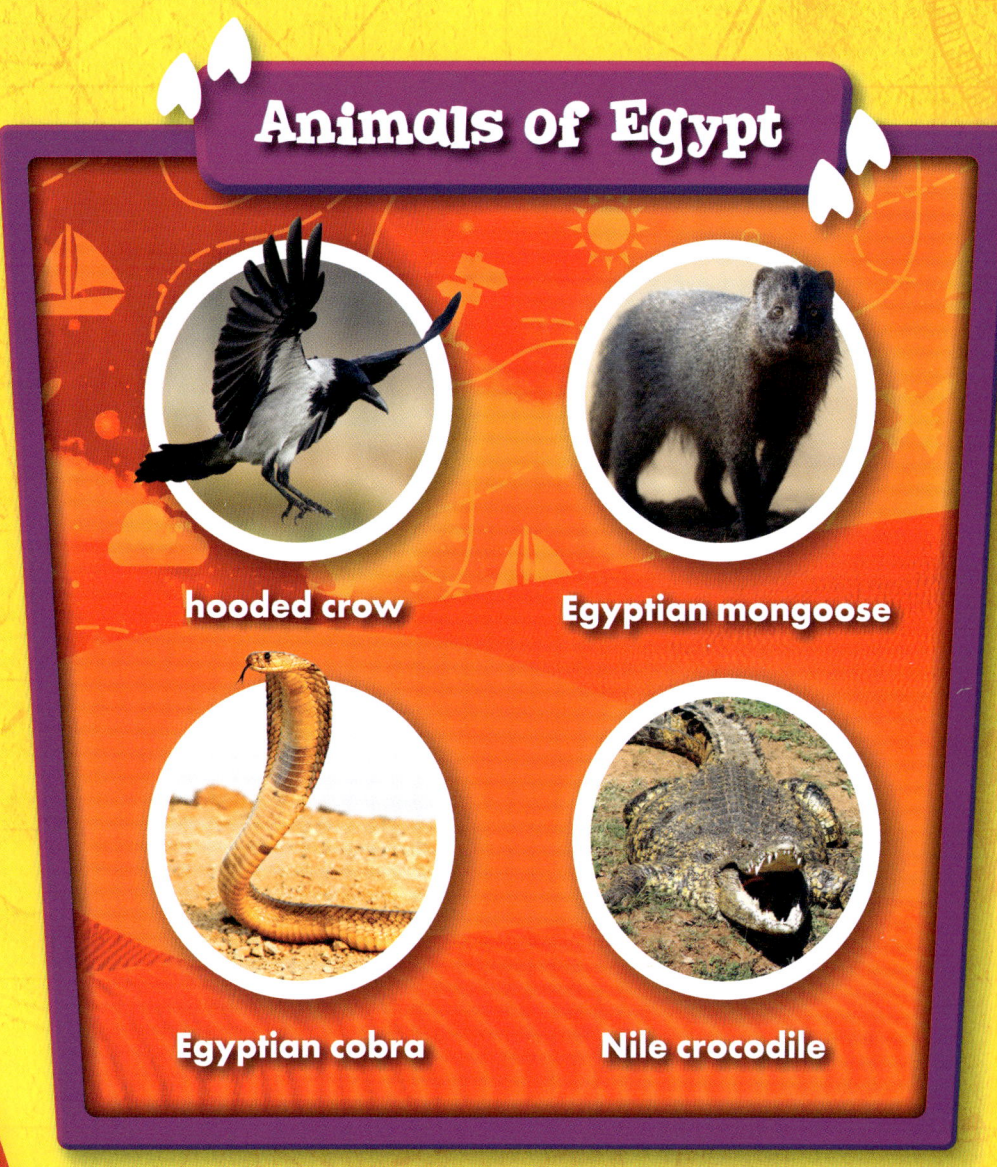

Animals of Egypt

hooded crow

Egyptian mongoose

Egyptian cobra

Nile crocodile

Egyptian mongooses fight cobras near the Nile River. Nile crocodiles swim underwater.

Life in Egypt

Most Egyptians are **Muslims**. Arabic is the country's main language.

Most people live close to the Nile River. Many live in villages.

soccer

weightlifting

People love soccer in Egypt. Weightlifting and wrestling are popular, too.

Egyptians enjoy boat rides on the Nile River. People also like games such as backgammon.

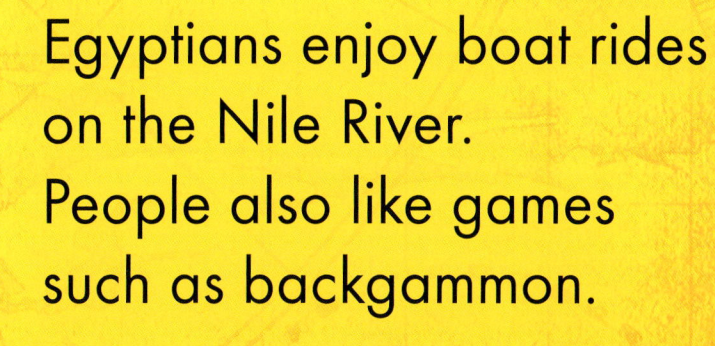

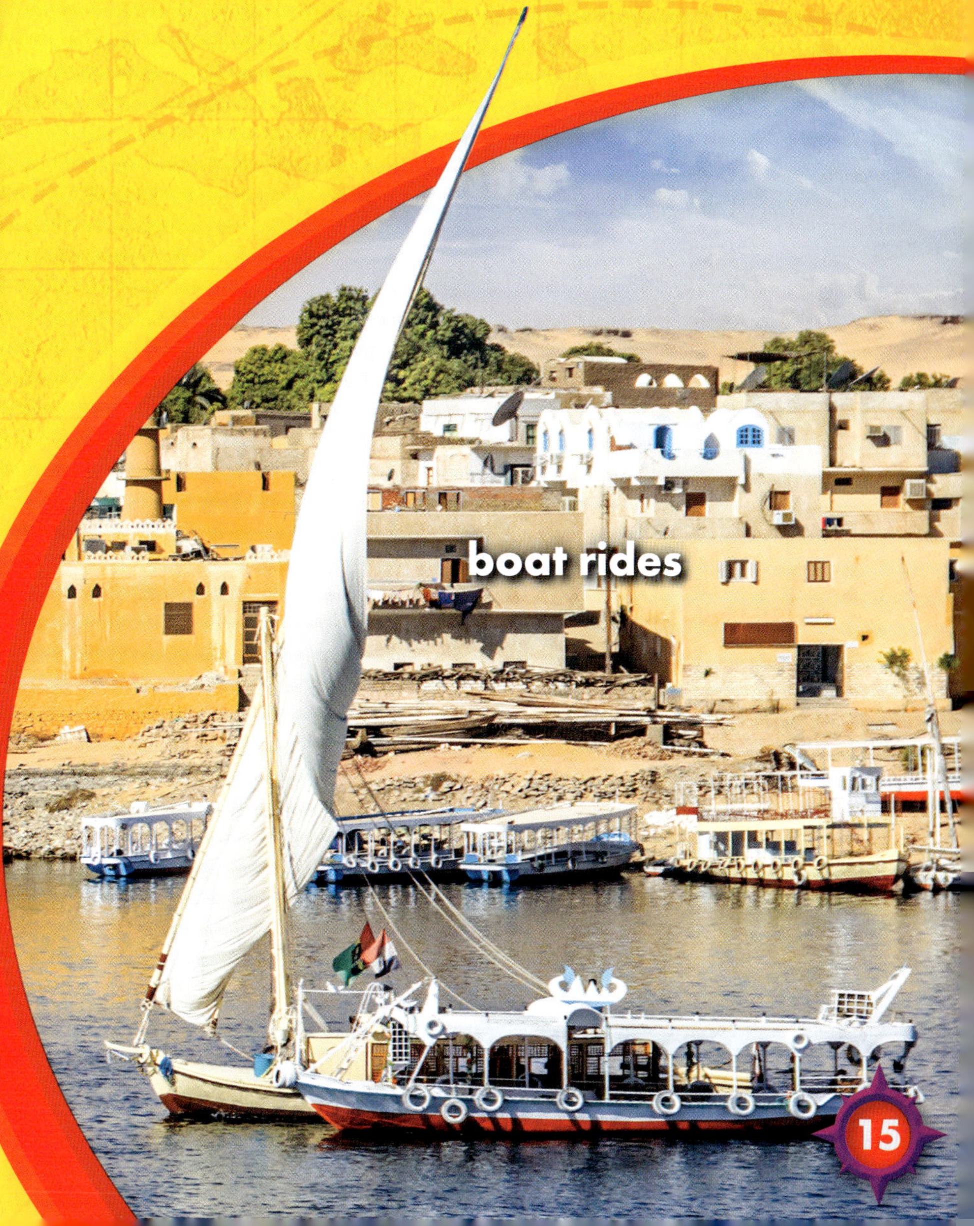

boat rides

Green *mulūkhiyyah* soup is a favorite dish. *Konafa* is a sweet treat!

Egyptian Foods

mulūkhiyyah soup

konafa

ful medames

falafel

Ful medames and falafel are also popular. They are made with fava beans.

Muslims honor Ramadan each year. It ends with *Eid al-Fitr*. Families come together to eat and pray.

Sham al-Nessim

Sham al-Nessim is a spring **festival**. Many holidays bring Egyptians together!

Egypt Facts

Size:
386,662 square miles
(1,001,450 square kilometers)

Population:
107,770,524 (2022)

National Holiday:
Revolution Day (July 23)

Main Language:
Arabic

Capital City:
Cairo

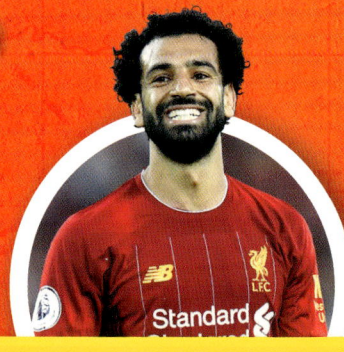

Famous Face

Name: Mohamed Salah

Famous For: soccer player who is the captain of Egypt's national soccer team

Religions

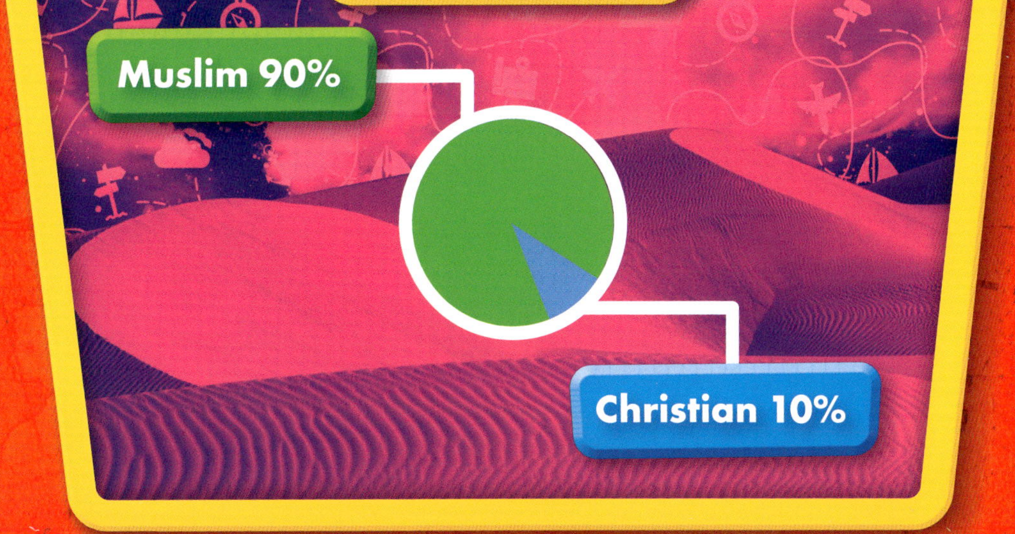

Muslim 90%
Christian 10%

Top Landmarks

Abu Simbel Temples

Great Pyramid of Giza

Great Sphinx of Giza

Glossary

civilizations—communities with set ways of life

deserts—dry lands with few plants and little rainfall

festival—a time or event of celebration

Middle East—a region of southwestern Asia and northern Africa; this region includes Egypt, Lebanon, Iran, Iraq, Israel, Saudi Arabia, Syria, and other nearby countries.

Muslims—people of the Islamic faith; Muslims follow the teachings of Muhammad as told to him from Allah.

peninsula—a section of land that extends out from a larger piece of land and is almost completely surrounded by water

sandstorms—events in which very strong winds blow sand around with great force in deserts

To Learn More

AT THE LIBRARY

Dean, Jessica. *Egypt*. Minneapolis, Minn.: Pogo, 2019.

Flynn, Sarah Wassner. *Ancient Egypt*. Washington, D.C.: National Geographic, 2019.

Meinking, Mary. *Let's Look at Egypt*. North Mankato, Minn.: Capstone, 2020.

ON THE WEB

FACTSURFER

Factsurfer.com gives you a safe, fun way to find more information.

1. Go to www.factsurfer.com.
2. Enter "Egypt" into the search box and click 🔍.
3. Select your book cover to see a list of related content.

Index

Africa, 4, 6
animals, 10, 11
Arabic, 12, 13
Asia, 6
backgammon, 15
Cairo, 4, 5
capital (see Cairo)
civilizations, 5
deserts, 6, 9, 10
Egypt facts, 20–21
Eid al-Fitr, 18
food, 16, 17
map, 5
Middle East, 4
Muslims, 12, 18
Nile River, 6, 7, 11, 12, 15
people, 12, 14, 15
rain, 9
Ramadan, 18
sandstorms, 9
say hello, 13

Sham al-Nessim, 19
Sinai Peninsula, 6
soccer, 14
summers, 8
villages, 12
weightlifting, 14
winters, 8
wrestling, 14

The images in this book are reproduced through the courtesy of: AlexAnton, cover, pp. 4-5, 21 (Great Sphinx of Giza); Alexandree, cover; Black Pearl Footage, p. 3; otorongo, p. 6; M. Timothy O'Keefe/ Alamy, pp. 6-7; Daily Travel Photos, pp. 8-9; Xinhua/ Alamy, p. 9; BearFotos, pp. 10-11; Marcin Perkowski, p. 11 (hooded crow); CORDEANT PHOTOGRAPHY, p. 11 (Egyptian mongoose); Hemis/ Alamy, p. 11 (Egyptian cobra); Karel Bartik, p. 11 (Nile crocodile); Jon Chica, p. 12; cinoby, pp. 12-13; Aleksei Smyshliaev, pp. 14-15 (soccer); REUTERS/ Alamy, p. 14 (weightlifting); akimov konstantin, p. 15 (boat rides); Iggi_Boo, p. 16 (*mulūkhiyyah* soup); Hashem Issan Alshanableh, p. 16 (*konafa*); Veliavik, p. 16 (*ful medames*); Paul_Brighton, p. 16 (falafel); John Wreford, p. 17; IBRAHIM EZZAT/ Contributor/ Getty Images, pp. 18-19; titoOnz, p. 20 (flag); Michael Regan/ Staff/ Getty Images, p. 20 (Mohamed Salah); Anton_Ivanov, p. 21 (Abu Simbel Temples); Merydolla, p. 21 (Great Pyramid of Giza); Sergei25, pp. 22-23.